Kristen Witucki

THE TRANSCRIBER

Kristen Witucki has been blind since birth and earned a BA in English from Vassar College, an MA in giftedness from Teachers College, Columbia University, an MFA in fiction writing from Sarah Lawrence College, and an Ed.M. in teaching students who are blind or visually impaired from Dominican College. She has been published on many blogs. Kristen Witucki lives in West Virginia with her husband, her son and her guide dog. Visit her on the web at www.kristenwitucki.com.

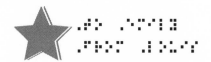

First published by GemmaMedia in 2013.

GemmaMedia
230 Commercial Street
Boston, MA 02109 USA

www.gemmamedia.com www.gemmaopendoor.com

© 2013 by Kristen Witucki

All rights reserved. No part of this publication may be reproduced
in any manner whatsoever without written permission from the
publisher, except in the case of brief quotations embodied in critical
articles or reviews.

Printed in the United States of America

16   15   14   13   2   3   4   5

978-1-936846-37-5

Library of Congress Cataloging-in-Publication Data
Witucki, Kristen.
   The transcriber / Kristen Witucki.
       pages cm. — (Gemma Open Door)
   ISBN 978-1-936846-37-5
   I. Title.
   PZ7.W788Tr 2013
   [Fic]—dc23

                                        2012045150

Cover by Night & Day Design

Inspired by the Irish series of books designed for adult literacy, Gemma Open Door Foundation provides fresh stories, new ideas, and essential resources for young people and adults as they embrace the power of reading and the written word.

Brian Bouldrey
North American Series Editor

**HELEN PLUM
LIBRARY
LOMBARD, IL**

GEMMA

Open Door

3 1502 00818 1495

For the family in which I grew:

In memory of my grandmother, Genevieve Schirm and my father, Chester Witucki;

For my mother, MaryJane Witucki;

For my siblings: Ed and Frances Farmer and Chet and Michael Witucki;

For my godparents, David and Vicky Schirm;

And for Emily Bubel and Kathy, Paul, Ken and Vincent Sieranski

ONE

Signs

On the strip of grass between the sidewalk and the street on the left side of my house, a sign stands, as if it were part of the land. It says: "BLIND CHILD AREA." There used to be two of these signs, one guarding each side of our house like soldiers. Now there's just one.

I asked Mom why we have to have signs telling the world that Emily is blind, or why we have to tell everybody we have a blind person living in our house. She said the town insisted on putting them up so that people who are driving too fast will see the signs, slow down and look to see if Emily is in any danger of being run over. But Emily's not stupid. If she wants to play in the street and get run over, that's her decision. She knows she's not supposed to play there, and if she gets killed by a car, that's her own fault, not the driver's. The sign also makes it seem like Emily is only allowed to play in the Blind Child Area, not in anyone else's space. What if a car hits her in someone else's area? Does that mean it's her fault, because she didn't play near the sign? Emily can't even see the darn thing! She knows where the signpost is, but she can't read the words. And what about me? I live here too! The sign should say, "BLIND CHILD AND SIGHTED CHILD AREA" or something. And if I'm playing in the street near the sign, is it OK for the driver to run me over?

You'd think, from the way it stands, that the sign will always be there, but that's not true. Like I said, there used to be two of them, one to the left and one to the right, both proclaiming the same message. Someone stole one about a month ago. I don't know why anyone would want to steal a sign saying "BLIND CHILD AREA." Who else in the world—besides us—needs a sign like that? If I had my pick, I'd steal "STOP."

But maybe there are people out there who collect signs, whose mission in life is to have one of every kind of street sign in the world. I can imagine my dad as a kid, collecting signs, or at least stealing one, but he'd never tell me if he did. Maybe someone in the world really needs "BLIND CHILD AREA" to go with "VILLAGE OF MINISINK HILLS," which hangs on the wall in our hallway, and "YIELD" and "KEEP RIGHT." Maybe that kind of collector steals signs from every country. I should find out what traffic signs say in Australia.

Perhaps there are sign-stealing competitions. "BLIND CHILD AREA" would score high in originality—there just aren't that many, so they must be collectors' items—but it would score pretty low in risk-taking. Whoever pinched it wouldn't have to climb out onto the median like they would if they were stealing a highway exit sign.

Or maybe there are people who don't want the drivers to know Emily is blind, who want someone to run Emily down.

TWO

Privacy

Emily is blind. She has never seen anything at all, not even when she was inside Mom. The thought of her eyes really not working took my brain a few years to absorb. When I was little, I kept looking for some evidence of cheating—an instant Emily would give up the game, open her eyes, and look at something. I remember telling her when I was about four that if she opened her eyes, they would start working. She said she tried that already.

When we were little, my sister was OK. She did color in my books, claiming she didn't know they already had words in them, and I cried. And she did pull all the pegs out of the Lite-Brite, so I had to hit her with the board a few times. But usually we had fun. We'd watch *Sesame Street* or *Mr. Rogers*. Sometimes we'd create a family with all our stuffed animals, her favorite game. Or sometimes we'd play my favorite, which was to pretend that the bed was an island, and you couldn't go into the water without being attacked by alligators. I would put my head way over the side of the bed and dare those alligators to hurt me, but Emily was too chicken. She'd huddle in a corner on the bed shivering. "Come down!" I would call out, but she'd tremble so much you would think she could see those alligators.

Then she started kindergarten. I was

still in preschool. Instead of playing with me, she'd hang out with stupid girls, and they would play dumb games with dolls, and I wasn't going to be caught dead with them. At first, I kind of wanted to find out what they were doing, but Emily would yell at me to go away, even though her friends didn't seem to care if I was around or not. So I hung out by myself and played with Matchbox cars or games on the computer.

But that wasn't good enough for Emily. She started saying, "He's invading my privacy!" So Dad put a lock on her bedroom door. The next day, when she and her friends were inside, I hopped on a desk chair like it was a bucking bronco and rode down the hallway, slamming against the door as hard as I could. Hi ho, Silver, away! Emily's room is right at the end of the hall—it's a straight shot—so I crashed hard enough to break the door open. The girls screamed, because the sound was so loud and unexpected, but as soon as Emily figured out what had happened, she ran toward me, her fists flailing in the air, knowing that if she covered enough airspace, she would eventually triumph. Her battle technique, while it was a waste of energy, was nevertheless effective. I jumped off the chair and ran away laughing, leaving it in the middle of the doorway to trip her. Behind me, I heard her wail like a siren, "Dad-dy!" I didn't laugh for long, because Dad made me pay for that door with my allowance forever.

Emily could lock herself and her

whole world in her room when she was in it, but if she was outside, the room was open to attack. One day, when she was at her piano lesson, I snuck into the bedroom. Her three favorite dolls were lying on her bed. Two of them were American Girl Dolls, a blonde-haired Pioneer and a brown-haired Victorian, eyes shut because they were lying on their backs, smiles identical, looking dressed up and helpless. The third was a baby boy doll, which my mom had gone to a lot of trouble to find. It was wearing blue pajamas, but I had seen its tiny penis once. I climbed up on Emily's desk chair and stowed the boy doll on top of a very tall dresser. After some thought, I ripped off his pajamas, leaving his plastic body exposed to the cold.

Then I hid each girl doll in a separate closet. Their eyes were startled open as I lifted them up, as though it was necessary for them to be awake when held. I didn't bother taking off their clothes, because they looked too complicated. I hung the boy doll's pajamas from the curtain rod. I held out a faint hope that my parents would blame Emily for not remembering where she had put her dolls. But when she ran into the dining room sobbing that her children were all gone, my dad immediately gave me a look. "She's so paranoid about being private she probably hid them and forgot where she put them," I suggested.

"You knew she wouldn't find them in the places you hid them!" Dad shouted after he had unearthed the dolls. "I know brothers and sisters fight," he added later when he calmed down, "but she can't see, and you can, so you shouldn't fight in a way that gives you an unfair advantage. If you have to fight, why don't you use your words instead? She's more than capable of reciprocating verbal attacks."

THREE

Miracle Child

Everyone thinks that just because Emily's blind, she's a walking miracle. But I know the truth. She's my sister, and she can't see, but she acts just like anyone else's older sister. She's a year and a half older than I am which, for her, means she can boss me around. But because she also happens to be blind, people think she's God. Or at least an angel. She has curly blonde hair and blue eyes like all of the angel pictures I've ever seen. I have straight brown hair and brown eyes.

I guess the teachers think of her more like a cross between an angel and a computer. What they say is, "She's amazing!" "It's so wonderful that she walks around all by herself!" And my favorite, "Why aren't you the student your sister was?" So I tell them things like, "What's amazing about walking?" "She's not a wind-up toy," or simply, "Fuck you!" Most of the time, I remember to save those kinds of retorts for inside my brain. I tried the last one out loud once and ended up in the guidance office. The counselor kept asking me questions about whether I ever set things on fire or dreamed about guns. Then she sent me back to the classroom after threatening to call my mother.

I returned home that night with a feeling of foreboding. My suspicion was confirmed when Mom asked me what happened at school today, and Dad looked like he was going to throw something. When I told her about the teacher's remark and the guidance counselor's weird questions, she said, "Louis, you will encounter a lot of stupid, annoying people as long as you are different from them or live with someone who is different from them, so you'll have to learn to ignore them."

"She's crazy," I thought. "How do you ignore people who try to mess you up?"

Dad took a sip of beer and gave me a frowning smile. "If you can't ignore them," he said, "at least stay out of trouble."

Only my fifth grade teacher assumed I was smart, but that was because she had

Emily in her class the year before. By the time I got there, she figured that if my sister was as smart as she was and blind, I must be a walking dictionary. If Ms. Lawson didn't know how to spell a word, she didn't look it up; she would ask me. At first, I dutifully told her how words were spelled, but one day, she asked me how to spell "cease." I had no idea, so I took a chance by spelling it with an "s" at the beginning. She believed me. Later that night, I looked it up and discovered I had got it wrong. So then I had lots of fun with my power over her, especially on the day I convinced her that Baltimore is the capital of Maryland. "Louis," she said, "your memory is unbelievable! I don't know what I'd do without you!" I've never been to Annapolis, but I feel sorry for the people who live there. So many people outside Maryland must forget about them.

FOUR

Transcribing

Don't get me wrong. I think some parts of being blind are pretty cool. For instance, I'm jealous that Emily gets to carry a weapon to school. If I had a cane, I'd want a sword inside of it, and I'd beat lots of people up with it. Sometimes if I tease her about B's on her report card or tell her she's fat, she hits me in the shins with it, and it really hurts.

Someday she will be old enough to get a guide dog, if she wants. You can't just use any old dog as a guide dog. They have to go through a lot of training and be really smart. If I was blind and had a guide dog, I'd teach it attack commands.

It wouldn't kill everyone, just the people who deserve it. I would teach it different degrees of attack: nip, bite, tear to shreds, amputate. And if the cops came, I would say, "Officer, I didn't see what it was doing."

Blind people have their own secret code, too: dot writing called Braille. I'm the only one in my family, besides Emily, who knows the Braille letters. At first, I would write Emily's name as Imely, because *i*'s and *e*'s are easy to reverse. So are *d*'s and *f*'s, or *h*'s and *j*'s, or *r*'s and *w*'s. And other letters I can't remember right now.

At first, I learned Braille so I could read her diary. Then I found out Braille has contractions, not words like couldn't and wouldn't and shouldn't, but tons and tons of abbreviations. Luckily, Emily's name doesn't have any, and mine only has one, the *ou* contraction. I didn't feel like learning them all, so I'll never know whether Emily writes about me and what she says. But I do like Braille. I can read it pretty well with my eyes, but when I run my hands across the words like Emily does, they just feel like a bunch of dots to me. I've become the family's Braille transcriber. I Braille all the birthday cards, the letters from Mom when Emily goes to camp, the Christmas tags.

And I'll never, ever forget the Christmas tags. I guess I was about seven, and my sister was eight. Mom came into my room where I was playing with cars by myself. I could hear my sister and her stupid friends laughing about something—probably laughing at me again—behind her locked door. Mom sat down on my bed Indian style, something I didn't see most adults do too often. Cupping her chin in her hand, she looked at me and said, "You know there's no Santa, right?"

"Um, yeah," I said. I kept looking at the Matchbox Ferrari I was trying to move around on the carpet so she wouldn't see how much her words surprised me. There were a lot of debates among my classmates about whether Santa was real. Some kids said he was just a story, and others insisted on his existence. I leaned toward the believers, because the idea was fun. What other guy in the world got to ride around with flying reindeer? It sure beat flying a plane.

Sometimes I thought about auditioning for the job when I grew up.

"Emily doesn't know that," Mom said.

"That's weird," I said. "She's older than me."

"Yes, but I wanted you to know first," Mom said. "I want you to Braille the Santa tags for me, so she can read them for another year."

"She's older than I am!" I repeated. "She should write tags for me!"

"Louis, don't be unkind," Mom said. "She can't read or write print."

So that Christmas, I struggled to fit the oddly shaped tags into the Brailler, to inscribe them with the name of an impostor, someone who could not even

Braille for himself . . . just like my parents. I felt like I was the first-born, not the youngest.

But it was Dad who blew the secret. "Joyce!" he cried out to my mom in surprise that morning. "You can really Braille!"

"Charles!" Mom shrieked. I don't often hear her raise her voice.

"I did it, Dad," I said. "Mom told me there wasn't a Santa." I could feel myself almost crying . . . almost. If I had been Emily, Dad would have kissed me, and I would have felt his scratchy beard against my face. But he just gave me a regretful look.

And Emily, amid her pile of presents, said, "Mom, really, who do you think you're kidding? I've known for YEARS there's no Santa. I was trying to protect Louis."

FIVE

Eye Shells

"Emily," Mom said, "your school picture looks awful!"

Surprised that Mom would say anything unkind to Emily, I said, "Ooooooo, let me see!" I was all set to make fun of Emily. Then I looked at the picture and gasped. Mom was right. I couldn't even tease my sister.

Emily started crying, ran to her room and slammed the door. Again.

"I know why it looks bad," I told Mom. "The photographer told Emily to open her eyes, and she did."

The photographer had stood by Emily longer than he did by anyone else, positioning her hands and shoulders just so as if she were bread dough he was kneading into shape. His voice had oozed like syrup—too sweet and too loud—and he had said, "Open your eyes more Emmy!" Emmy? I felt sorry for Emily all of a sudden. How could she possibly know opening her eyes like that made her look like a ghost? Her eyes looked like canyons in her thin face— too wide, too plastic, too empty. I could take a better picture than that.

Emily's real eyes are not developed. She wears plastic shells like thick contact lenses that give her eyes shape and color. They're called prostheses, but at home we just call them eye shells. When I found out Emily could have whatever color eyes she wanted, I told her, "You should get purple eyes."

"That sounds pretty." she cooed.

I realized she liked my idea too much, so I tried again. "No, I know," I told her, "you need snake eyes."

"Ew!" she shrieked. "Snakes are slimy!"

"No, they're not," I told her. "Worms are slimy. Snakes feel cool and dry."

"Ew!" was all she said.

SIX

Cigarettes

"Louis," Emily said one day, "help me write a letter."

"You know how to type," I told Emily, "so write it yourself." And she did know how to type. She has been typing fast since she was seven or eight. At first she had a really cool-looking manual typewriter, but later they gave her an electric one that made a pretty nice clatter once she got going. Sometimes Emily's ink would run out in the beginning or the middle of what she was writing, and when one of us told her most of her work was blank, she would cry.

"I am going to type the letter," said

Emily with great dignity, "but what should I write in it?"

"What are you writing about?"

"I'm writing:

Dear Daddy,

Please stop smoking, because you're the best daddy in the whole world, and I love you as much as I love Mommy.

Love, Emily."

"That sounds OK, I guess, but it won't work. It's probably better if you do something bigger like break his crystal ash trays into a thousand pieces or flush his cigarettes down the toilet."

"But then I'd get in trouble," said Emily, "and I hate getting in trouble."

"Nah," I said, "they would think it was me anyway."

"You would tell them it wasn't, and they'd look at me and know you were right," Emily conceded. "I can't lie. My face always gives me away."

"What gave you this letter idea anyway?"

"The Smokeout campaign at school. The teacher said we should tell our parents to quit or else write letters to them, and they would quit if they knew how much we loved them."

"He loves us," I said, "but he has to want to quit. I asked Mom when I was a little kid, 'What are you doing that for?' and she quit that second. But she was ready to quit. Dad isn't. He smokes lots of them. He even smokes with the patch on."

"He might be if I give him this letter. I'll Braille it, too."

"He can't read Braille."

"I know, but then it looks like I put in twice the amount of effort. Didn't your class hear that, too?"

"Hear what?"

"About the ways to help your parents to stop smoking."

"I wasn't listening," I admitted. "I was thinking about . . ."

"How could you not listen? It's so important!"

"So write the letter," I said, "but it's not going to change anything."

Emily sighed.

"Don't worry," I told her. "Dad will take care of us. That's his job."

SEVEN

Ballerina

Emily went through an art phase when she was about ten. She was sure she would become a famous sculptor. Maybe she thought someone would see her sculptures and think, "Wow, she did that and she's blind? Even though it's crap if a sighted person did it, she's blind, so it's great!" And she was really into the ballerina idea. She couldn't dance, but she had heard of this sculpture by Edgar Degas, a sculpture so beautiful and fragile that she couldn't touch it in the Philadelphia Museum of Art—she could only stand in front of it and feel jealous of the people who could see it. So she got this idea that she could make the next ballerina, the one everyone could touch. She sat at her desk in her room for hours, her door casually open for the admirers who would parade by. But there was just me. "What's that?" I asked her, but I knew already.

"It's a ballerina, stupid!" she said.

I looked down at it. The legs were straight sticks and looked like the dancer couldn't walk, much less move her body gracefully. The body was as flat as a cutting board. And her arms stuck out to the sides like she was trying to fly away from her creator. I guessed the perfectly round little ball was her head. Her tutu looked like a pancake in the middle of it all, and it was made of clay, not real lace. Emily did get her clay hair braided correctly, though. "She doesn't seem very happy," I told Emily, for once not wanting to say anything too mean.

"I'm not happy either!" she shrieked and squashed the dancer, stuffing her remains into a drawer.

"Yes, you are," I told her. "You seem happy all the time."

"Yeah, I guess, but this dancer makes me miserable."

"You can't be her."

EIGHT

Falls

I wonder what blindness is like. When
I close my eyes, I still see. And I know
my sister doesn't just see black like everyone thinks. She doesn't see anything.
That's hard for me to explain, because
it's hard for me to understand. When
Emily traded me in for her friends, I
was bored. I started trying to be blind.
First, I walked around with a T-shirt tied
over my eyes, but then that got too hot,
so I just walked around with my eyes
squeezed shut. I slammed into walls,
and once I even walked off the top of
the stairs, because I hadn't seen them. I

landed with my left foot doubled back under me, and I limped around for a few days. But eventually, I began to understand how Emily could sometimes walk around without touching the walls. Each area of the house had its own echoes. I could hear the closed-in sound of the hallway and the way the echoes opened into the kitchen and the living room. I could hear more reverberation as I approached the kitchen, because there was no carpet to muffle its sound. I could hear the smallness of my room against the bigness of Emily's—she got more space, because her Brailler and books took up so much room.

I began to walk around with my eyes closed all the time, and at night, I refused to turn on the lights. "See, Emily?" I'd tell her inside my head. "I'm better at being blind than you." And I was better, I thought, except for that fall down the stairs . . .

One day, I led Emily to the edge of a little wall which was too high, and I told her to step down. She tripped and fell hard on her hands and knees on the concrete. As blood poured from the wounds, she gave me a look of genuine surprise before she started to cry. Then I understood that Emily had not seen that drop, that she would always be blind, and even though I could walk and write like a blind person, I could see when I wanted to see. When I had fallen off the stairs at home, I had chosen to fall. I knew then what Dad meant about unfair advantages, not that I could see and she couldn't, but that I was using my sight to trick her.

I was twelve when I led Emily to fall, and after that, I never hurt her unfairly again. True, I did punch out at her on occasion if she hit me first, but most of my punishing instinct was satisfied by teasing her. All I needed to do was point out that her stomach was too big, or she was stupid, because she got one B on her report card, and she would immediately become indignant or weepy. She'd yell back that I was even stupider, just because she got more A's than I did or because they let her into the high school band as an eighth-grader. My favorite retort was "Shut up," even though I knew it didn't say much.

Our parents started changing, too, becoming more extreme versions of the people they were when we were little. My mother was gentle, always patient, and forever standing up for my father, who could scare you silly just by yelling. He always smelled like cigarettes those days, and I had to take the recycling bin of beer cans out more and more often.

I remember one Friday night attempt to spend quality family time at a restaurant. Emily, who was always impatient to get going, was outside, waiting next to the van. Dad saw her through the window, ran outside and started yelling, "Don't touch that! Stop leaning on that goddam car door!"

I wondered what the hell he was

talking about. Emily was just standing next to the van. Were my eyes making it up? So I ran outside and started yelling myself, "Stop hollering at her! She's not even touching the damn car!"

"You shut up and mind your own business!" he shouted back.

We didn't go out that night. After she had finished comforting Emily, Mom came into my room and told me, "Dad has been having these mini strokes, TIA's. Maybe he just had another one of those."

"I don't care," I told her. "He shouldn't yell at her about something that doesn't even make sense."

"Try to think about someone besides yourself for a change," was all she said.

I thought Dad needed to think about

someone besides himself for a change, and I told her so.

"You don't know anything about what's really going on," she told me. Then she sighed and walked out of the room.

I hadn't known about the mini strokes. All I knew was that every once in a while, dad went nuts. I had also observed, though Mom never told me, that his foot had been bothering him for a year or more. After my fall on the stairs as a blind person, I had limped around for a few days, but the pain had worn off. It was hard for me to understand why Dad didn't just recover in the same way. I'd watch his steps become more and more unsure. Yet he refused to get a cane or crutches or a wheelchair. "The doctors can't do anything," he would say and would grab another cigarette or open another beer.

It seemed to me that while my sister was disabled, he was crippled. She had been born with the disability, but it wasn't just because she came into the world with it; she had also made it part of her life. Emily must have been about six feet tall by then, and she was already playing trombone solos for the high school band, already winning music awards. Sometimes she really nauseated me. Or maybe I was just annoyed with those teachers who would never have noticed Emily's talent if she weren't blind. I wondered if having a younger blind marching musician got the high school band more points, what the judges said in the box out of range of the audience's hearing. Or in their range, for that matter. "Look at that blind one go!" I wondered if Emily's trying so hard was pointless, because no matter what she did, whether she failed to do something or whether she exceeded people's expectations, they would always notice her blindness first.

In fact, the band was so good that year that they got to go to a championship for the best bands in the tri-state area. They won third place, and they got home so late at night that the principal let them all come into school late the next day.

Dad had another doctor's appointment, so he told Mom he'd take Emily to school. Then he surprised me. "I'm not driving over there twice," he said. "You can go in late, too." I felt like a rebel, a celebrity, as Dad tore over to the school, pedal to the metal. I didn't tell him I was missing a history test

When we got to the school, I jumped out of the car. Kids were loitering outside between classes, and I didn't want to be seen with my dad or my blind sister anyway, so I ran toward the school as fast as I could, leaving Emily behind. I almost reached my friends when something told me to turn back. I didn't see them behind me, so I reluctantly began to walk back toward the car.

"I'll help you to the door," Dad was insisting.

"No," said Emily, probably just as embarrassed about having a parent with her as I was by her. "I know how to do this. I come here every day."

"I don't care," Dad told her, his tone rising. "I'm helping you."

Emily must have decided it was better to risk humiliation about walking with her parent than to risk said parent flying off the handle about nothing, so she got out of the car, put on her backpack, folded her cane and held out her hand to take Dad's elbow. Instead, he grabbed her arm, and I could see he was leaning heavily on Emily for support. He walked slowly, and Emily trembled under her backpack of books, her trombone in its case and his weight on her arm. I started to call out to them, started to walk over to help my dad, even though I don't know what I would have done if I had gotten there—push him back toward the car? Get on the other side so the two of us could walk him to the school, then walk him back? But he saw me and looked at me with more anger and more despair than I had ever seen in him.

At that moment, the warning bell rang, and one of Emily's girlfriends came over. "Hi, Emily," she said, then turned to my dad. "We have the same class anyway," she told him, and he nodded at the girl, accepting her explanation as he let go of Emily. Emily and the girl disappeared inside, and I waited a minute. Dad sat down on a bench by the school. The late bell began to ring, and I still had to turn my note into attendance. I left him on the bench, left him to figure out how to get back to his car alone.

NINE

Treading Water

I remember the first time my dad lied to Emily in front of me. When I was seven, he decided to take me with him on a plane trip to Iowa to see our uncle and aunt.

"Can I go?" Emily asked.

"No."

"Why not? It's not fair!"

"We can only afford two tickets, so I'm taking Louis."

On the plane, Dad told me that he didn't want to take Emily to see his sister and brother-in-law, because he felt frustrated with their sympathy. They kept telling him his family was in their prayers, as though his family was totally isolated from them. "She's not helpless, you know," he would say on such occasions, but they still wanted to pray for him. He had decided not to bring Emily along, to hide her from what they might say.

As it was, I wished Emily had gone instead. They were boring. The weekend activity was fishing. Dad taught me how to put worms on the hook, how to assemble the line and to reel in a fish, but the days were long, hot and filled with mosquitoes. While we waited for hours, Dad taught me the rhyme:

Fishie, fishie in a brook,
Daddy caught you on a hook.
Mommy fried you in a pan.
Louis ate you like a man.

"Was I a man for not killing the fish?" I asked, but Dad didn't know.

For dinner the first night, my aunt and uncle ordered pizza, but it had anchovies on it. (The second night, we had fish, of course, from a lake, not the ocean, like at home.) They didn't listen to Rock 'n' Roll either. Plus, they figured that if Emily didn't come, it was because she couldn't travel, because she couldn't see, and it would be too hard for her. I know that's not true. Emily is always talking about how she wants to go to places like Ireland and Japan and Kenya, and I know she'll do it, too.

Several years later, though, the summer Dad started getting sicker, Emily and I did spend time with Aunt Ruth and Uncle Bob at their summer house near the Finger Lakes. I wondered which finger their lake was on, thought about how Emily was always using her fingers to read Braille or to play the trombone. Emily and I took an aged canoe out on the water one foggy summer morning. I peered into the lake fog ahead, feeling, for the first time, blind. I paddled with caution. Emily took off boldly into the water, into the mist quilting our faces. She had an odd expression of being at home which I couldn't understand. And in that euphoria, she leaned to the side, tipping the canoe and us into the water. I felt myself hit the lake before I could make out the boat some inches away. We were both wearing life jackets. "Emily, you tipped it!" I yelled as I grabbed the canoe which had somehow righted itself once released of its burden of irresponsible young boatpeople.

"I didn't tip it!" she yelled back.

I wanted to argue, because I knew I was right, but I called, "Here, take my paddle and hold onto the canoe. I'll swim us back to shore." I was, after all, the male, the sighted one. It reminded me of the times Emily colored in my books and pulled pegs out of my Lite-Brite. It reminded me of riding the tandem bike with her. All she needed to do was pedal. I had to steer us, to pedal, to carry whatever it was we needed or wanted. Emily could relax, could even wreck things, but I had to fix them. I swam and swam, but even though I kicked hard, and Emily was treading water, the waves kept pulling us further away. I heard a distant motor start, knew my uncle and aunt were coming to rescue us in their old rowboat, the children from this other family who had landed like aliens in the middle of their summer haven.

"Louis," Emily said, "at least this will be something to write about." And I wished I had not given her that canoe paddle, because I wanted to hit her over and over and over again.

The rowboat showed up, and my uncle and aunt pulled me up first. As they did, the canoe flipped and landed upside down over Emily who was still treading water and holding the paddles. I heard her cry out and saw the canoe assume her panic, twitching as she thrashed underneath. I regretted having wanted to hurt her. I could hear the choppy waves as she must have heard them then, like the sound of a shell pressed to an ear turned static. "Get her out of there!" I yelled at my uncle and aunt as they strategized and argued from the safety of their boat. "Goddamit, get her out of there!"

TEN

Begging

The day before our Christmas break from school began, Dad told Emily and me he needed to go to the hospital for an operation on his leg. "I thought the doctors couldn't do anything," I said.

"Well, we'll see," he said. He promised he would be home for Christmas. "Be good, and help your mother." Emily came into the rec room where I was watching *The Simpsons* and told me that Dad would be all right. "I know that," I told her. But I had seen the expression on his face when he said we would see.

Dad had a heart attack in the operating room, as though his heart waited until he was surrounded by machines and medical staff to give out. I imagined my attack guide dog ripping at Dad's chest from the inside. I wanted to go see him, but my mom said I couldn't. "I can't drive you home when you get bored or sad and want to leave. I have to stay there with him," she told us, "so stay here, and try to relax on your Christmas break." Easy for her to say, because I had four school projects to do that week.

The days developed their own routine. Mom would wake the two of us up around six in the morning. We'd eat breakfast in silence, and I'd pour myself a cup of coffee from the pot. I knew something was wrong when Mom watched me do it but said nothing. I'd dump about half the sugar bowl into my cup to try to cover the bitter taste. Mom would take a shower and dress as though she was going to work, but she was only going to the hospital. She would tell us what food was in the refrigerator or would leave us money to order pizza. By seven, she was out the door, and Emily and I were on our own. I watched a lot of TV. Emily stayed locked in her room with a book. If I banged on her door, she ignored me, and I wondered if she slept, because it was easier than worrying. Mom called once in a while to check on us, but she wouldn't come home until two or three in the morning, and then she'd just fall into bed. Many days, I didn't see her at all. Instead, I would hear the muffled bang of the front door from my bedroom.

On Christmas, the day Dad was supposed to come home, I waited up for her, because I wasn't sure whether she needed me to Braille Emily's tags and how many she needed. I realized later that it would have been easier to just Braille out several of them, but I wanted to stay awake in defiance of kid rules, to watch as the clock hands signified the shift from Christmas Eve to Christmas Day, to witness Santa's not coming, to find out if it would snow. It didn't. But kid rules prevailed. I fell asleep in the rocking chair and was awakened by the front door slamming shut. "Mom," I said, stretching, "what about the Christmas tags for Emily?"

"They amputated Dad's leg," she told me.

"They what? They cut his leg off? But a heart attack doesn't make your leg hurt."

"I don't know. I guess they weren't really watching his leg after the operation, or maybe it didn't work. Anyway, he had blood poisoning, and they said it could spread if I didn't let them amputate it. So I told them to do it."

"How do they do it? Do they use a saw?"

"Jesus Christ, I have no idea! I didn't watch them do it! And don't tell your sister. I shouldn't have told you, but you were up."

"What about Emily's tags?"

"Don't worry about them. We'll tell

her which presents are hers. I didn't have time to buy much. And I don't think Santa will show up."

"I already know there's no such person."

Mom sighed. "I forgot."

"Can I come with you to see Dad in the hospital?"

"I stay there for a long time each day. You'll get bored."

"I know. I'll bring a book or a game or something. But I want to see him."

"All right, if you want. Now get to bed."

Later that morning, we hurriedly exchanged presents, and Mom went to the hospital alone, promising me before she left that she would come home that night to cook dinner, and she'd take me back with her that night.

We drove to the train station and rode the rest of the way into Camden on the Speedline. Through the windows of the train I could see the abandoned factories and row homes whose broken windows had jagged stares. The buildings that were inhabited looked run-down. But Our Lady of Lourdes Hospital was a graceful structure, wide at its base, tapering like a tower as it touched the sky. "Mom, who's that dude on the top of the building?" I asked her.

She gave me a quizzical look. Then she laughed. "Mary wasn't a dude, exactly."

"Oh."

I was surprised to see that the hospital,

which had seemed spacious from the outside, had hallways full of clutter—spare medical equipment, IV poles, upturned beds. As I walked around, leaving my mom in the ICU to talk to the doctors, I discovered a chapel whose windows sparkled in a thousand million different hues as light from street lamps poured through them. They would be even more beautiful in the daytime on a sunny day. A few people were in the chapel, some praying, some sitting still. A woman cried quietly. None of them talked to each other. I gathered that it was a place for the privacy of grief.

When I returned to the ICU, Mom was alone beside Dad's bed. He lay absolutely still, stiller than I had ever seen him. He was connected to machines that monitored his pulse and breathing. Occasionally, lines on the screens would shift. An IV on one stand dripped blood into him. He was covered by a blanket which was pulled up like a tent around the place where part of his leg used to be.

Mom pulled up a folding metal chair on the far side of the bed and motioned for me to sit. She began to talk to Dad, but I didn't understand why, because his eyes remained closed. I didn't know at the time that people believe patients sometimes still hear words in a coma. She told me to talk to him, too, but I didn't want to. I didn't know what to say. My tongue felt thick, my throat parched, and I was sure that all the water in the hospital could not slake my thirst.

I began to feel drowsy. It wasn't just

hearing my mother's voice, talking on and on about nothing and everything. The air, smelling of disinfectant and decay, had a lulling quality, a dried-out, heavy feeling, as though it was pushing me back into the chair. The more closely the air pressed in around me, the more distant I felt from my father. It was as if he and the entire room were tilting away from me. And I thought, my dad will not die, but he won't come home the way he left, either. He won't have part of his leg. And there was no fighting the weight of that realization.

In my dream, Dad became a beggar. He took the train into Philadelphia, bought a reduced fare ticket. He got off the train at 30th Street Station and hobbled carefully up each step on his crutches, reminding me absurdly of a toddler who must put both feet on each step. He got himself out to the corner of Market Street. Even though it was snowing heavily, set up a folding metal chair, then carefully spread his whole leg and his half leg out for people to see, and he put a cup down beside him to collect money. A woman in jeans and a Hard Rock Café sweatshirt came up to him. She introduced herself as Mary, and I was surprised that she wasn't wearing a robe like the statue on the top of Lourdes. "Mary?" I asked her. "I thought people weren't named Mary anymore." "Stay out of this," she told me, "you don't understand what's really going on." She asked Dad what he was doing there. "I can't walk anymore," he said. "I'm not normal anymore." Mary seemed to give the comment some thought. She looked at his neat work suit, one pant-leg pinned up, at the worn dress shoe he wore on his remaining foot. "What you need," she said, "is a pair of boots. Well, one boot, actually." She disappeared into the crowd, and my father was left alone. Some people threw coins in his cup, averting their eyes. Others hurried past, not noticing him or pretending not to notice him. Then Mary was back. She held out a shoe box from Nordstrom's. "How did you know my size?" my father asked her. "Because this isn't real, and you are normal," she said, "but think about that later, and just hurry up and put this on, or your other foot will be so cold that it will need to be amputated, too."

"Are you okay?" my mom asked me. "Louis, are you all right?"

I lifted my head from the hospital floor. It hurt a little, but I felt normal. "I'm okay," I said, sitting all the way up. "I guess I fell out of the chair. Next time I want to fall asleep I'll sit on the floor first."

It was all Mom could do to convince the nurses that I didn't need to stay in the hospital for observation. She got an ice pack to put against the goose egg on my forehead and told me it was time to go home.

"It seemed like you were dreaming about something," Mom said on the train home.

"I don't know," I lied. "I guess I dreamed his leg grew right back, like a lizard's." I didn't want to tell her that Dad had really shrunk in my dream.

ELEVEN

Daydreams

I always had trouble imagining death. I often played with toy guns with my friends, and I'd usually die in a battle at least once. If we were in the pool and they were water guns, I would fall onto my back in the Dead Man's Float. I would relax into the water, assured that it was all a game anyway. But sometimes at night, I would lie in bed, trying to be dead. I could stay absolutely still. I could even stop breathing. But how could I not think?

Once when I was younger, Emily caught me in my attempt at death. I was

lying on my back on the unmade bed,
running sneakers still on my feet. I lay
absolutely still and held my breath. But
I couldn't stop thinking. "Think about
nothing," I told myself, trying to imagine the water in the pool being absolutely
still. "But that thought," I thought, "is
a thought."

"Louis?" Emily called. "I need you to
read something!" Her voice sounded little and far away through my ringing ears.

"Louis?" she called again. I kept holding my breath.

"Louis!" she yelled. Now she was
right near the bed. I jumped, and my
breath came out suddenly. I was trying
not to hear her, trying not to open my
tightly clenched eyelids.

"Are you asleep?" she asked me.

Dammit, I thought. "No," I told her, "I was trying to be dead."

"What?" she said. "To kill yourself?"

"No, I was just trying to be dead."

"That doesn't make any sense," she said. "How can you be dead if you don't kill yourself?"

"There are other ways to be dead."

"Well, lying still isn't one of them," she said. "Can you help me with my homework?"

The next day, we went through the same routine. Mom went alone to the hospital for the day, then came home to cook dinner and take me back with her at night. She asked Emily if she wanted to go, but Emily didn't want to. "Your dad has septic poisoning," my mom related to me in the car. I had no idea if she gave Emily updates, and if she didn't, why she had decided to fill me in. I thought of septic heating systems and wondered if septic poisoning made my father feel cold.

I sat on the same uncomfortable metal chair. Wondering if my dad was cold made me feel sad, and a few tears fell, so I lowered my head, hoping my mom wouldn't notice them. I still didn't want to talk to him. This time, when I started to feel sleepy, I kept my promise to my mother and slumped down to the floor in front of the chair.

As my head fell forward onto my folded arms, I daydreamed about what life would be like if Dad were a pirate with a peg leg. He would sail on a ship from island to island, seeking buried treasure. Instead of a parrot, he would have a guide dog named General, except the dog wouldn't guide but would sniff out the places where the treasure was hidden instead. Eventually, Dad would get so much treasure that he could take over one of the islands. The people on the island would make him a king, and they all would be amazed that, even though he had a physical challenge, he could still find all this treasure. He was amazing! General was amazing! My amazing dad would hobble up to accept his crown, wearing a flowing silk robe and carrying an amazing gold cane with a sword inside it. The people would stand around their conqueror looking, well, amazed.

TWELVE

Emily

When we got home, Emily asked me how Dad was doing. "Come to the hospital, and see him yourself," I told her.

"I don't want to."

"Why not?"

"I don't know," she said. "Just tell me how he's doing."

"Fine," I lied. "Isn't a septic system supposed to heat things?"

"No, stupid," she said, "it has something to do with eliminating waste in remote areas."

"Waste?"

"The stuff from people's toilets."

The next morning, Mom told Emily

she better come along with us that night, because she didn't know how much longer Dad would make it. Emily got pale. "But you said he was all right!" she accused me after Mom left us alone.

"He is all right," I said. "He's alive."

"But you told me he is all right!"

"Well, he's not all right anymore."

"I didn't want to talk to him if he couldn't talk back."

"But he might be able to hear you."

"It doesn't matter. It would be like he's not there anymore if he's not talking. He won't yell anymore. He won't pretend I need his help anymore."

"You're right about that," I said. "He'll be helpless, because they cut his leg off."

Immediately, regret burned my throat.

Mom had told me not to tell Emily, and I had broken that promise.

Emily stood still for a minute or two. "They what?" she said finally.

"They chopped off his leg, and that was supposed to make him better. But it didn't make him better, and it won't grow back."

"I hate you!" Emily exclaimed with tears in her eyes, tears that would not fall. "You're a liar!"

"You're the one who said he wasn't going to die," I said. "Well, you're not as smart as you think you are. Just because you're blind doesn't mean you know everything."

Emily was no longer pale. Her face turned red with anger, and I knew I had made her feel much worse than I would have if I had told her that her tits were too small or that she was stupid and ugly. She looked like she wanted to hit me, but she didn't. Instead she said, "Just because everyone thinks it's amazing that I move around doesn't mean that I think I know everything. And you lied to me. Mom and Dad lied to me. All of you are horrible. He's not all right!" Then she burst into tears and ran to her room, slamming the door behind her as hard as she could.

I stood and stared at Emily's closed door. I wished I had a desk chair to slam it open with, but I was too old for that. She had shut me out.

As we drove to the hospital that night, Mom told us that our uncle and aunt from Iowa were coming tomorrow, and then I knew it was bad.

When we got to Our Lady of Lourdes, Mom took Emily in with her to talk to Dad first, leaving me outside in the waiting room. When it was my turn to go in, I said, "Hi Dad" without thinking, figuring he probably couldn't hear me. His eyes fluttered open for a second, then closed again. Maybe he *could* hear me. I touched his shoulder which was exposed above the white blanket. His skin felt cool and dry. But seeing his eyes open for that moment was encouraging, so I kept talking. "Dad," I told him, "when you come home from the hospital, you'll learn how to move around in a wheelchair and on crutches, and then once you learn how to do those things, you'll go back to work. And maybe it won't be totally the same. Maybe they'll move your office so that you don't have to walk so far. But you won't need to beg for money or be a pirate, because you have a desk job anyway." I paused, thinking. "And maybe someday they'll give you a fake leg, and then you'll fool everybody, and no one will think you're crippled. But even if they think of you that way, it won't really matter, because you can still work, and you can still take care of us."

When I came out, Mom left me with Emily and went into talk to Dad by herself.

"What did you talk about in there?" I asked Emily.

"Oh," she said, "what it would be like when he came home, that he'd still be OK with a disability. What did you talk about?"

"Really?" I said in surprise. "I talked about the same thing."

To keep from crying, we laughed.

When my uncle and aunt arrived the next morning, they did not tell my mom that her family was in their prayers, and they didn't seem to care that Emily carried a cane to the airport with her. Instead, they told Mom that they would keep us home with them while she went to the hospital, and we would make Christmas cookies. At least the cookies would come in time for the new year.

As I took the last cookie sheet out of the oven, the phone rang. I picked it up. "Tell Ruth and Bob to come to the hospital," Mom told me. She said that Dad would be dead soon. Well, that's not exactly what she said. What she said was, "Dad's not going to make it, so they should see him." I didn't ask her why she couldn't just say he would be dead. I didn't ask her why she didn't want us there. I had already seen him. Instead, I hung up and delivered the message.

As I watched my uncle and aunt's rental car pull away, I wondered if lying to my father about his homecoming would put me in hell forever. But I hadn't really lied to him, just as he hadn't really lied to me when he told me he would come home. I had lied to myself that he would get better, even as I knew he would die. Lies to myself are the hardest kinds of lies to reverse. And I guessed that if he were dead, he wouldn't need to think about how to live with a disability. He wouldn't yell anymore. He wouldn't feel depressed. Instead, Emily would travel the world and live her life without fanfare. But what if my dad's body had not betrayed him so that he slept until he was dead? What if he had woken up angry, depressed, forced to live? Perhaps he would have struggled a little longer, then decided to try to move in a world which tells you that walking needs two legs. And then I knew death, not as the moment when a person no longer breathes or thinks but as the moment time disappears.

Acknowledgments

I am fortunate to have more friends and mentors than I can properly acknowledge in such a small space. My brother, Chet, inspired much of this story. Carolyn Ferrell and Lucy Rosenthal offered support and guidance during the early drafts. Joan Silber called my attention to the Gemma Open Door Series and remains a valuable writing mentor and friend. Trish O'Hare got into the heart of this story and helped me to change it into a real book. Stacia Brown and Nicole Haroutunian eased my panic with their final, final reading of the manuscript. Anannya Dasgupta took my author photographs, and Sheila Amato provided the gift tag picture. My husband, James Simmons, loves me profoundly and never complains when I need to disappear with my words for a while. My son, Langston, has shown me the fountains of renewal inside myself as he greets the world with anticipation and delight.